W9-DCZ-422

cloverleaf books™

Community Helpers

TWINSBURG LIBRARY
TWINSBURG OHIO 44087

Let's Meet a Construction Worker

Bridget Heos

illustrated by **Mike Moran**

J
624.
Heo
[Blue dot]

M MILLBROOK PRESS · MINNEAPOLIS

With thanks to my husband, Justin,
and Mr. Lee Moore —B.H.

To Robyn and Jordan —M.M.

Text and illustrations copyright © 2013 by Lerner Publishing
Group, Inc.

All rights reserved. International copyright secured. No part
of this book may be reproduced, stored in a retrieval system,
or transmitted in any form or by any means—electronic,
mechanical, photocopying, recording, or otherwise—without the
prior written permission of Lerner Publishing Group, Inc., except
for the inclusion of brief quotations in an acknowledged review.

Millbrook Press
A division of Lerner Publishing Group, Inc.
241 First Avenue North
Minneapolis, MN 55401 U.S.A.

Website address: www.lernerbooks.com

Main body text set in Slappy Inline 18/28.
Typeface provided by T26.

Library of Congress Cataloging-in-Publication Data

Heos, Bridget.
    Let's meet a construction worker / by Bridget Heos ;
    illustrated by Mike Moran.
        p.   cm. — (Cloverleaf books: community helpers)
    Includes index.
    ISBN 978-0-7613-9023-7 (lib. bdg. : alk. paper)
    1. Building—Juvenile literature. 2. Construction workers—
Juvenile literature. I. Title.
    TH159.H46 2013
    624.092—dc23   2012019101

Manufactured in the United States of America
1 – BP – 12/31/12

TABLE OF CONTENTS

Chapter One
Trucks with Teeth

Our class is taking a field trip! We're visiting a **construction zone.** Mr. Moore greets us. He is the boss here. He's going to show us how construction workers build a new building.

He says we have to stay outside the fence.

Workers only in a CONSTRUCTION zone!

Construction workers are people in the community. A community is a group of people who live in the same city, town, or neighborhood. Some construction workers work on buildings. Some build roads. Ironworkers, concrete workers, carpenters, roofers, and plumbers are all construction workers.

This isn't just any construction site. It's our **new school!** But right now, it's mostly dirt.

"Awesome!" Aiden says. "We can play king of the hill at recess!"

Mr. Moore smiles. "All this dirt will be flat. You'll have a playground on top."

We see lots of **trucks**. Some work with **big metal teeth**. Some have **strong arms**.

An excavator digs wide ditches for basements. It digs narrow ditches called trenches for water pipes. It also moves dirt for making roads.

The trucks don't do all the work. People are inside. They steer. They guide **heavy loads.**

Chapter Two

Safety First!

Mr. Moore used to be a **carpenter**. He helped build things with **wood**. Later, he was the lead carpenter. Now he is the leader of all the workers.

He follows plans that an **architect** created. Together, the workers turn those plans into a building.

Construction workers take classes and get training to learn how to do their jobs. They may start work as apprentices. That means they learn on the job from other workers.

11

Mr. Moore's number one job is keeping people safe. He makes sure workers wear **hard hats** to protect their heads.

They wear orange **safety vests** so others can see them easily.

Beep! Beep! A concrete mixer beeps as it backs up.

Beep   Beep   Beep

The beeping helps keep everyone safe. Workers know to move out of the truck's path when they hear it.

Wet concrete flows through a long pipe to the ground. This will be our school floor.

Drivers must get the concrete to the construction zone quickly. Concrete begins to dry after about ninety minutes. Then it becomes hard. It won't pour.

"Will we sink into it?" Luke asks. Mr. Moore says the concrete will **dry** and **harden**. Then carpets and rugs will go on top of it.

Chapter Three

Green School

Some workers work high above the ground. **Masons** build the walls with **bricks**. Someone runs wires for **electricity** through the walls.

Crunch! A few bricks break.

They will be **recycled.** So will leftover metal, wood, cardboard, and concrete.

"Your school is a **green** school," Mr. Moore says.

Amia asks, "Apple green or forest green?"

"Not the color green," he says. "Green means it's **Earth-friendly**."

He unrolls our school drawing. **Solar panels** on the roof will take in **energy** from the **sun**. This energy will power our computers, lights, and more.

SCHOOL

Big windows can also make a building Earth-friendly. Windows and skylights let in sunlight. So people don't always need the lights on. That saves energy.

We can't wait for our sunny, green school to be finished.

CALL

Because Mr. Moore lends a hand to **build** our new school, *we* give *him* a hand!

Make a Graham Cracker House

You can construct your own building with graham crackers and peanut butter. Try to stand the walls up straight. Seal off any cracks where outside air could get in. The best part is that you don't need to recycle broken or leftover materials—you get to eat them!

What you need:

4 graham crackers (rectangular)
a bread knife (with a jagged edge) for a grown-up to use
peanut butter (or cream cheese, in case of peanut allergies)

a butter knife
a large, flat cutting board
mini pretzel sticks
mini shredded wheat squares

What to do:

1) Take two whole graham crackers. Ask a grown-up to use the bread knife to saw the corners off one end of each cracker. One end will still be square, and the other half will be pointy like a triangle.

2) Break (or saw) two more crackers in half so that you have four squares.

3) Use the butter knife to spread peanut butter (or cream cheese) along the bottom and both side edges of one pointy graham cracker. Do the same to all edges of one square cracker.

4) Line up the edge of the square cracker with the matching edge of the pointy one. Stick them together in an L shape, standing up on the cutting board, to form two walls.

5) Spread peanut butter along the edges of the other pointy cracker. Attach it to the standing square to form the third side. Do the same to another square cracker and attach it to complete the walls.

6) Spread peanut butter just inside the edge (in a U shape) on one side of the last two square crackers. Place these on the top edges of the house to form the roof.

Make a Graham Cracker House (Continued)

If you want to help your house save energy, place a pretzel stick in the space at the top of the roof to seal it. Spread peanut butter on one side of the shredded wheat squares, and stick them to the roof to keep outside air and rain from getting in. Add one-quarter of a graham cracker as a door. Then decorate it as you like!

GLOSSARY

apprentice: a worker who is learning how to do a job from a more experienced worker

architect: a person who designs buildings. An architect creates the plan that builders will follow.

concrete: a mixture of cement, sand, gravel, and water

concrete mixer: a truck with a spinning drum that holds and mixes wet concrete

construction zone: an area in which buildings are being built, knocked down, or repaired

Earth-friendly: not harmful to water, land, or the air

energy: usable power from any resource, such as the sun, wind, oil, or coal

excavator: a construction vehicle with a scoop attached to an arm. It is used for digging and moving dirt.

green school: a school with Earth-friendly building features

recycle: process used materials to make them like new materials for another use. Saving used materials to reuse them later is another kind of recycling.

BOOKS
Harris, Nicholas. *A Year at a Construction Site.* Minneapolis: Millbrook Press, 2009. This book's illustrations show how workers build a school from start to finish over a year.

Hudson, Cheryl Willis. *Construction Zone.* Cambridge, MA: Candlewick Press, 2006. Photos take readers into the action as workers and machines build a huge building at the Massachusetts Institute of Technology.

Zemlicka, Shannon. *From Rock to Road.* Minneapolis: Lerner Publications, 2004. Learn how construction workers use bulldozers, dump trucks, and other machines to make smooth new roads.

WEBSITES
Green Schools Initiative
http://www.greenschools.net
How green is your school? Take a quiz to find out, and learn how to make it greener.

Fun Jobs
http://www.kids.gov/k_5/k_5_careers.shtml
Find out about many different careers. Which jobs have you seen people doing in your community?

LERNER SOURCE™
Expand learning beyond the printed book. Download free, complementary educational resources for this book from our website, www.lernersource.com.